To Mummum

M.M.

For Han with love
D.A.

COME BACK SOON
by Miriam Moss and Dawn Apperley
British Library Cataloguing in Publication Data
A catalogue record of this book is available from the British Library.

ISBN 0 340 85415 4 (HB)
ISBN 0 340 85416 2 (PB)

Text copyright © Miriam Moss 2003
Illustrations copyright © Dawn Apperley 2003

First edition published 2003
10 9 8 7 6 5 4 3 2 1

Published by Hodder Children's Books
a division of Hodder Headline Limited
338 Euston Road London NW1 3BH

Printed in Hong Kong

Miriam Moss • Dawn Apperley

Come Back Soon

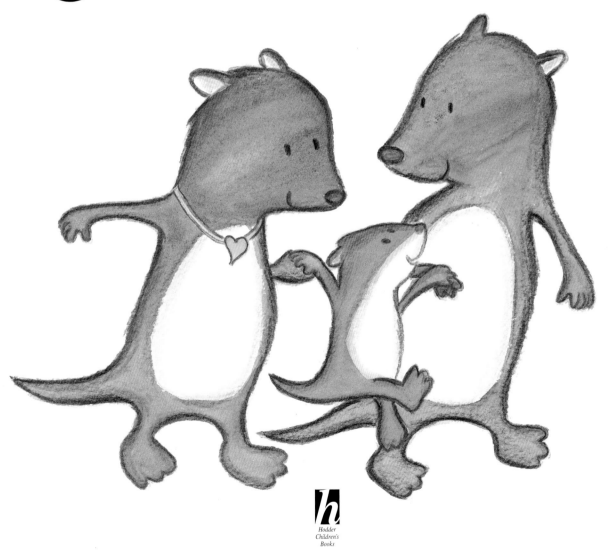

Hodder
Children's
Books

A division of Hodder Headline Limited

Little Ollie picked the letter up off the doormat.
Then he ran upstairs and jumped back
into bed with Mum and Dad.

'How nice to have you back,' said Mum,
snuggling him.
'I always come back, don't I?' smiled Ollie.
'You do,' laughed Mum.

'Dear me,' said Dad, as he read the letter.
'What's the matter?' asked Mum.
'Uncle Oscar has hurt his leg. He wants
you and I to help him out for a day or two.'
'And me,' said Ollie.
Dad hugged him. 'You must stay
here, safe with Grandma.'

Mum and Dad packed their rucksacks
while Grandma made breakfast.
'When will you come back?' asked Ollie.
'Tomorrow,' replied Mum.
'When IS tomorrow?' asked Ollie.
'After just one sleep,' said Mum.

It started to snow. Ollie and Grandma
watched the world turn white.
'We'll be able to make a snow den later,'
said Grandma.

Mum and Dad kissed them goodbye and set off.
'They'll be back soon,' said Grandma.

Suddenly Ollie jumped off Grandma's knee. 'Mum! Dad!' he cried, as the snow whirled in. 'When will you come back?'

Mum kissed Ollie again.
'We'll be back tomorrow,
after just one sleep,'
she said.
Then she pulled off
one of her gloves.
'Will you look after this
for me,' she asked,
'until I come back?'
Ollie nodded.

After they had gone, Ollie put
Mum's glove on.

It helped him to brush
his teeth and tidy
his bed.

Then, while he (and the glove) stirred Grandma's cake mixture, she sang to them.

'Mum gave you her glove to keep, Till she comes back after just one sleep.'

The glove went everywhere with Ollie that day.

Together they jumped along in Mum
and Dad's footprints…

...slid down
snow hills...

...and skidded on the frozen lake.

Then they built a snow den, filled it with treasures and had tea in it.

At bathtime the glove watched from a safe place
while Ollie raced his boats…

…until Grandma came in.

'Goodness, what a mess!' she said, helping Ollie into a towel. 'You'd better run and get a cloth before I read you a bedtime story.' 'You have to sing me the glove song too,' said Ollie.

The next day, Ollie woke early and looked out of the window. But there was no sign of Mum and Dad! Even their footprints had vanished. 'Grandma!' cried Ollie. 'I've had one sleep. Where are Mum and Dad?'

'They'll be back in time for lunch,' called Grandma.
'Come and help me make it.'

While he was putting the bowls out, Ollie
sang Grandma the glove song.

'Mum gave me her glove to keep,
Till she comes back after just one sleep.'

Suddenly they heard the
crunch of snow outside...

...and there were Mum and Dad!

'You came back!' said Ollie.
'We always do, don't we?'
smiled Mum.
'Yes,' said Ollie. And
while they were hugging
him, he took the
glove off.

'You can have this back,' he said,
'now I've got you!'

GROLIER

B O O K S

Grolier offers a varied selection of
children's book racks and tote bags.
For details on ordering, please write:
Grolier Direct Marketing
Sherman Turnpike
Danbury, CT 06816
Att: Premium Department
GUK

My a Book

by Jane Belk Moncure
illustrated by Pam Peltier

THE CHILD'S WORLD

Mankato, MN 56001

Little  a had a box.

He said, "I will fill my  box ."

Little a put on his hat and
went for a walk.

He found
apples,
apples,
apples.

He put the apples into his box.

Little  found an alligator.

He put the alligator into his box.

Little  found ants, ants, ants.

"In you go, ants," he said.

Then Little  found arrows,
arrows,
arrows.

Did he put the arrows into his box?

He did!

Little a found an axe.

It was a toy axe.

He put the axe into the box.

Now the box was so full …

the ants,

the arrows,

and the axe
fell out.

The apples and

the alligator

fell out too.

"Who will help me
fill my box?" said Little a.

An astronaut came by.
"I will help you," said the
astronaut.

"We will fill your box."

Then the astronaut

took Little  for a ride.

25

Up, up, and away!

ants

alligator

arrows

astronaut

apples

axe

More words with Little

antelope

acrobat

antlers

anchor

animals

ambulance